FRED

SNUFFLENOSE

and the

Baby Ducks

RICHARD MILLER

MILTON & HUGO L.L.C.
4407 Park Ave., Suite 5
Union City, NJ 07087, USA

Website: *www.miltonandhugo.com*
Hotline: *1-888-778-0033*
Email: *info@miltonandhugo.com*

Ordering Information:
Quantity sales. Special discounts are granted to corporations, associations, and other organizations. For more information on these discounts, please reach out to the publisher using the contact information provided above.

Library of Congress Control Number:	2024925410	
ISBN-13:	979-8-89285-369-9	[Paperback Edition]
	979-8-89285-370-5	[Hardback Edition]
	979-8-89285-371-2	[Digital Edition]

Rev. date: 11/27/2024

Frederick Cornelius Johann Snufflenose was worried. For the past two weeks he had been very worried. Fred Snufflenose worried a lot. And, when he worried, his nose ran. He was well suited to his name.

But Fred Snufflenose was worried today.

He and his best friend, Phil Erup, had found a mother duck lying on a nest of seven eggs. The nest of seven eggs was under a bush. The bush was beside the wall of a great, large church that stood proudly right in the center of town. The church was very large and very busy, and Fred Snufflenose (for that is what people called him) was worried that someone from the very large and very busy church would scare the mother duck away from her nest of seven eggs. Not on purpose, mind you, but possibly by accident. So, Fred Snufflenose and Phil Erup had decided to keep the duck's nest a secret.

Each morning, Fred Snufflenose and his best friend, Phil Erup, (for that is what Fred called him) got out of bed, got dressed, and walked from their house on Fence Street to the very large church which was right in the center of town, to see if the mother duck was still sitting on her seven eggs. One brilliantly sunny spring morning – it was a Thursday – they began their walk. They walked faster and faster, because Fred was feeling more and more worried than usual.

When they got to the bush beside the very large church in the center of town, Fred Snufflenose took one look at the nest and said "Oh! OH! OH DEAR! The seven eggs have hatched and everyone is gone."

Indeed, the seven eggs HAD hatched. They were split down the middle and their rounded part rested on the ground while the sharp cracked edges pointed up. They were empty.

"Everyone is gone," Fred Snufflenose repeated. He began to worry again. Now he was worried that the seven baby ducks had not gotten safely to the creek. The creek was rather far away, after all.

"Gone," echoed Phil Erup, "but where and how?"

"I do not know," said Fred Snufflenose. "But I think I will go and look for them." Phil Erup said "Good luck Fred Snufflnose. I am going back to our house on Fence Street to drink some coffee," and they said good-bye to each other.

Fred Snufflenose walked past the very large church in the center of town, and he started climbing up and then down all the very large steps to the very large church, and then he crossed the busy main street. He crossed the street very carefully, looking right and left, but he did not see any mother ducks or baby ducks in the street. He kept walking down the path that led to the creek. When he got to the creek, he stopped and looked in and thought. And thought and thought.

The water was clear. It was a bit too deep, and it was moving very fast. It went splish-splash against the many rocks. "I think this would not be a very good place to bring seven baby ducks," he said. "They would struggle in the fast-moving water going "splish-splash" and might go "wham-slam against the rocks. And oh! Oh! OH DEAR! That would be absolutely horribleiffic."

Fred Snufflenose said funny words when he was upset, because his emotions got into his brain and his mouth and floated around in them until a strange word came out.

He turned and walked up the creek a bit toward some very old buildings. One of them had a sign out front that said "Tannery."

"Oh!" said Fred. This is one of the very fine buildings that are part of our very fine Historical Society. "And look," said Fred to no one in particular, for there was no one there. "Beside the Tannery is what is left of the city's very first butchery. Fred Snufflenose knew about the very first butchery because his fifth great-grandfather was the very first butcher! He had come across the ocean on a boat that was not very large, from a place called Silesia, and that had been the start of Fred's family in America.

Across the lane from the butchery foundation was the grist mill, where the grain was ground into flour. There he saw a lady and her two little girls. Both little girls had blond hair. "Hello," said Fred Snufflenose. "Have you seen a mother duck with her seven baby ducks?"

"My name is Ruth," said the littlest girl. "I have a pet guinea pig. Her name is Daisy."

"That is very interesting," said Fred Snufflenose. "But, have you seen any ducks today?"

"NO!" shouted both girls, who then said they were sorry for shouting. Their mother led them in another direction, and Fred walked on.

Fred Snufflenose was even more worried now, but he kept looking. He walked on to the little stone bridge that crossed the creek. He stood in the middle of the bridge and looked one way and then the other way. When he looked one way, he saw that the water was very choppy. When he looked the other way, he saw that the water was much calmer. "A mother duck would put her babies in the calm water," he thought. There were no ducks in the calm water, but there was a large black bird , sitting on a low hanging branch and drinking water.

"Have you seen any baby ducks?" Fred Snufflenose asked the large black bird. The large black bird looked at Fred rather oddly, but did not say anything. "Of course not," Fred said to himself. 'Everyone knows large black birds cannot answer questions."

Fred Snufflenose turned back the way he had come. As he walked, he looked hopefully and carefully into the creek but no ducks were to be seen. He thought he should walk beside the stream now, and look in the stream while he walked.

So, he turned and walked back through the very old park, past the very old buildings, until he got to a very new bridge over the creek. This led to a parking lot where a truck was parked. Inside the truck, a man was sitting and looking at his phone.

"Hello," said Fred Snufflenose. "Hello, yourself," said the gruff man. "OH!" thought Fred. "He does not seem very friendly."

"Have you seen any baby ducks with their mother?" he asked the gruff man. "I have been sitting in my truck and looking at my phone. No, I have not seen any baby ducks and I have not seen any ducklings either!" the gruff man replied in an unhappy tone.

"Oh MY," thought Fred, "he is definitely not very friendly, and besides, I ought to have known that baby ducks are called ducklings." But Fred Snufflenose, even if he had unkind thoughts about some things, was a kind and patient man. And so, he said to the man "Yes, you are correct. I have been calling them baby ducks, but I really should call them ducklings. Thank you for pointing this out to me. I will stop saying baby ducks and start saying ducklings." After he said this, the man smiled at Fred and said "I hope you find the ducklings. It seems to be important to you."

Fred walked a little farther along the side of the creek until he found a nice grassy path that went right into the creek. "This would be a good place for ducklings to get into the creek," he thought, but when he looked into the creek, he saw many Canada geese right where the ducklings might have gone into the creek. Some were sleeping on the bank, some were preening their feathers on the bank, some were standing in the creek looking all around them, but none of them were actually swimming in the creek.

"Oh! OH! Oh DEAR!" said Fred Snufflenose. "I do not like Canada geese. They always hiss at me and honk at me and flap their large wings at me, and make a terrible fuss. No, I do not like Canada geese. I like Canada people, but not Canada geese." So, he did not bother to ask them if they had seen the mother duck and her seven little ducklings.

He walked on, along the bank of the creek and came to the street that went past the University. Here, the creek went under the street and there was a nice bridge to hold the traffic. Fred Snufflenose crossed the street and walked to the middle of the bridge. He could see part way down the creek.

Something to his left moved in the creek. It was a papa duck. He did not know whether the duck would answer him or not, and he asked "Oh, please, Papa duck, do you know where the mother duck and her seven ducklings are? Are you their Papa?" Papa duck did not say anything, of course, but he DID give Fred Snufflenose a knowing look. And then he turned away and started to swim on down the creek.

"Oh! OH! Hmmmm," Fred Snufflenose said "I wonder…"

"But," he thought, "I am getting very tired from all this walking and looking and worrying, and I am getting very hungry for my lunch, and I am a long way from my home on Fence Street. I shall walk just a wee bit farther and try to find the mother duck and her seven ducklings, because I am even more worried about them than I am tired or hungry.

He walked on, and tried to see into the creek, but he could not see anything. The trees and the bushes were so thick along the banks of the creek.

In a short time, he came to a bend in the road and at that place, he could stand on the sidewalk and see into the creek. There stood his friend, Phil Erup at the railing of the next bridge over the creek. "Look," he called, "Here is a mother duck with seven little ducklings. I think we have found them."

"Oh," said Fred. "Oh, OH, OH...HERE THEY ARE! Aren't they beautiful? Aren't they wonderful? I am so happy we found them. Now I can walk home to my house on Fence Street and have my lunch."

"And you can stop worrying!" added Phil Erup.

"Yes, I can! I can stop worrying.' And so that is what Frederick Cornelius Johan Snufflenose did!